HORSE
MEETS
DOG

By
Elliott Kalan

Illustrations by
Tim Miller

BALZER + BRAY
An Imprint of HarperCollinsPublishers

Balzer + Bray is an imprint of HarperCollins Publishers.

Horse Meets Dog

Text copyright © 2018 by Elliott Kalan

Illustrations copyright © 2018 by Tim Miller

For information address HarperCollins Children's Books, a division of HarperCollins

Publishers, 195 Broadway, New York, NY 10007.

www.harpercollinschildrens.com

Library of Congress Control Number: 2017954056

ISBN 978-0-06-279110-8

The pictures in this book were made with brush and ink and digital hocus-pocus.

Typography by Dana Fritts

18 19 20 21 22 SCP 10 9 8 7 6 5 4 3 2 1

❖

First Edition

To Danielle and our Sammy,
who help me figure out what I am

—E.K.

For Donna and Dana.
Thank you for all of it.

—T.M.

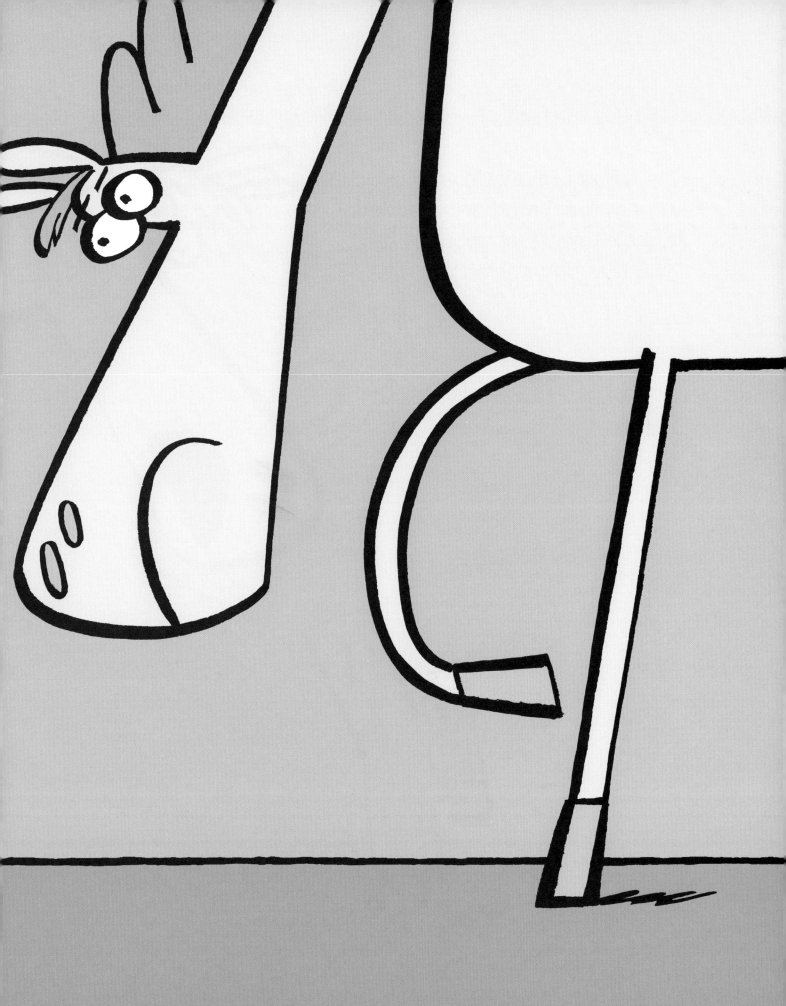

You are mistaken. I am not big. I am normal-sized. In fact, I was just about to tell you that you are very small.

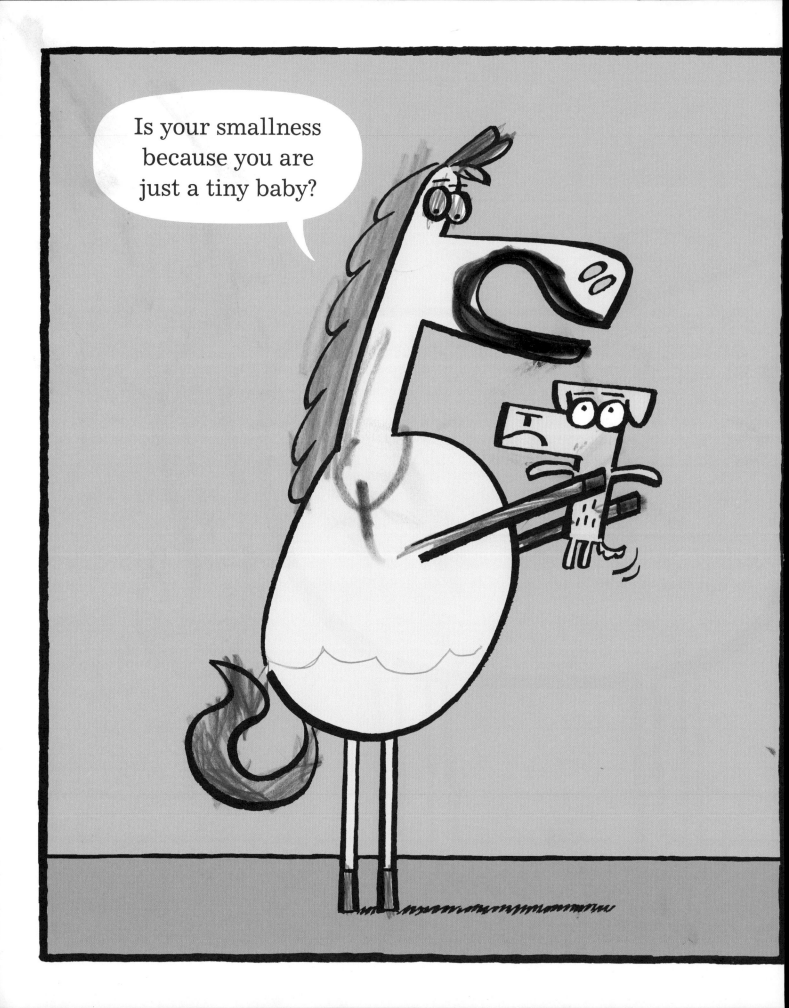

Aww, look at this wittle cutie tiny baby! Does Tiny Baby need a bottle of hay?

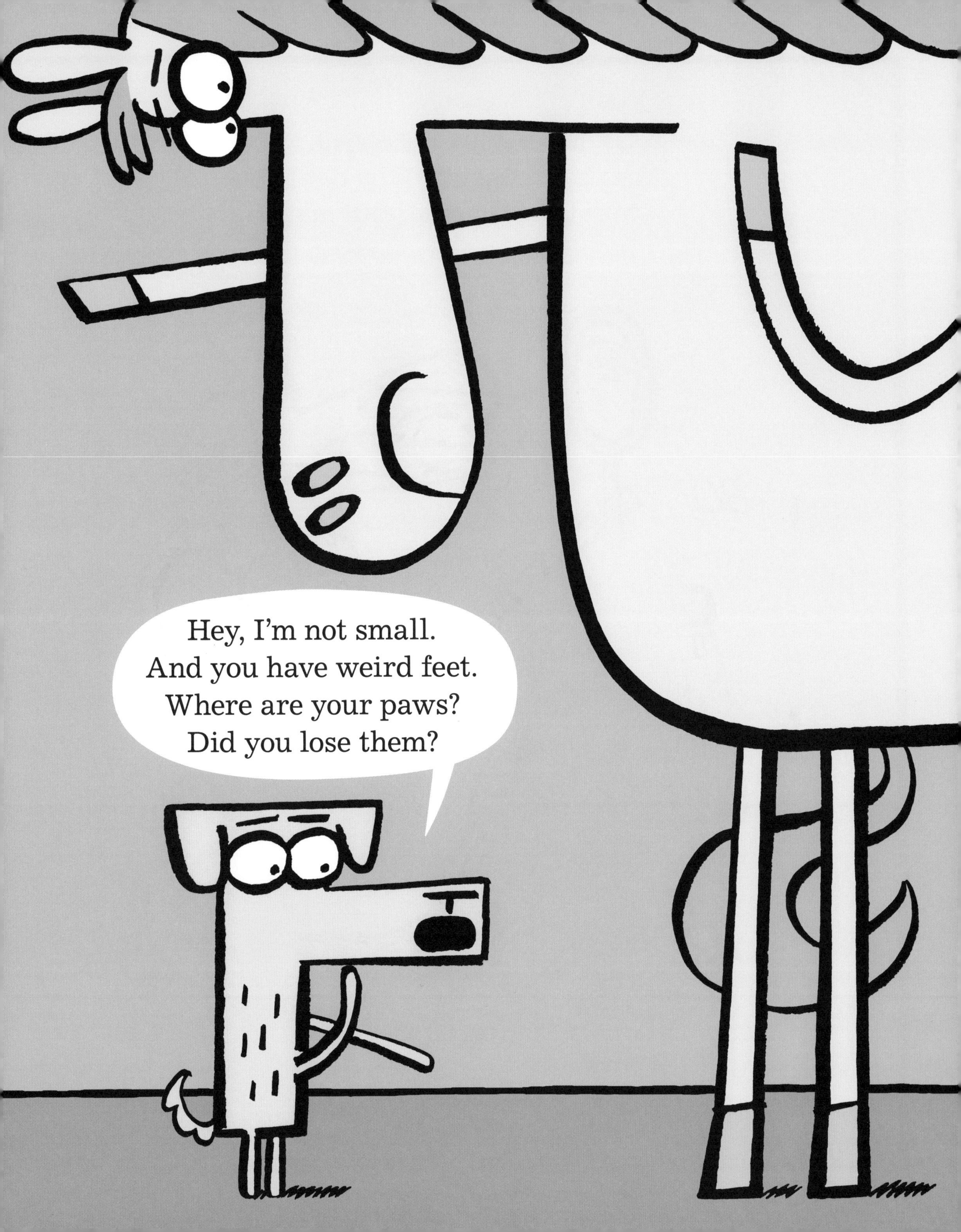
Hey, I'm not small. And you have weird feet. Where are your paws? Did you lose them?

Also, your tail sticks up. It should hang down, like a gorgeous hair waterfall.

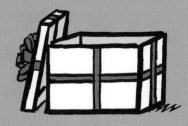

Someone sits on you, and you take them wherever they want to go. Fun!
That doesn't sound like fun to me.
Oh, but it is. SO MUCH FUN.

Excuse me? You threw it. You go get it.

No, this is how it works: you go get it, then I throw it again, and you go get it again.

What kind of horse are you?

What kind of dog are you?

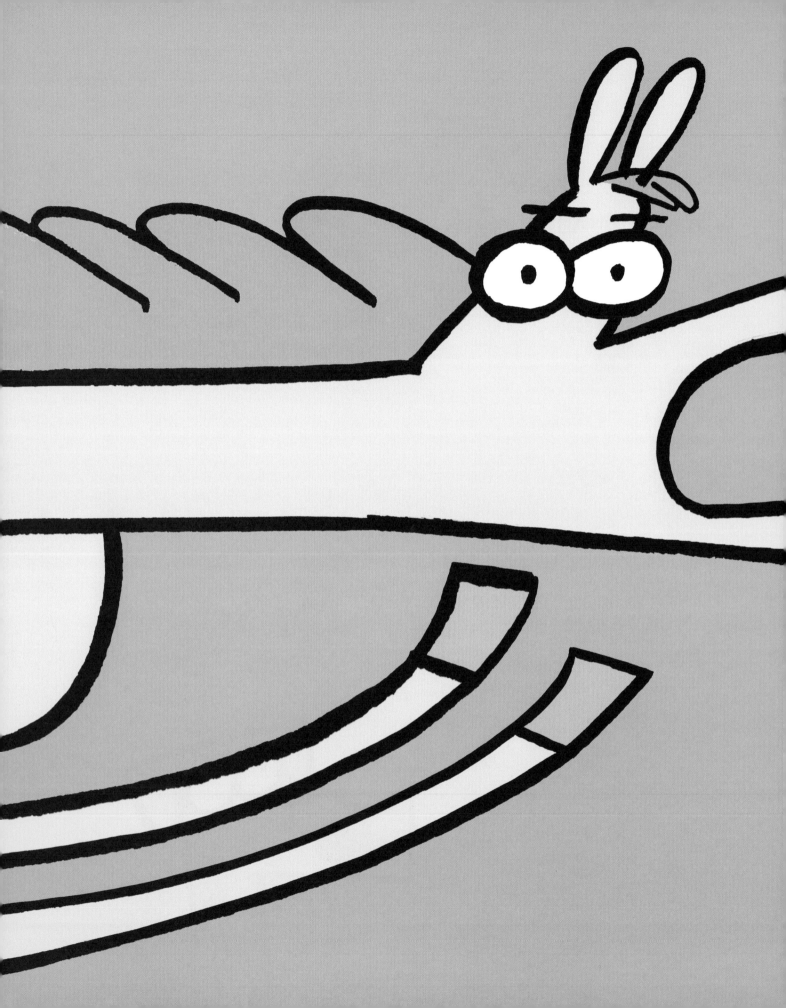

Are you sick, Tiny Baby Horse? Because something is seriously wrong with your whinny.